FIRST BOOK OF GERMANY

Hans Peter Thiel

English text by Heather Amery and Sandy Walker

Illustrated by Ilse Ross

Contents

With thanks to Paula Borton

Looking at Germany

This book tells you about Germany, which is the fifth largest country in Europe. You can see from the map on this page how varied the scenery is in different parts of the country. On the next few pages you can discover the different regions of Germany and what you can see there. Later on in the book you can find out about how German people live, what they enjoy doing and how they celebrate special occasions.

Rivers and lakes

Germany has lots of big rivers and lakes. Some rivers are linked by canals so ships can sail from one river to another.

The longest rivers are the Rhine, the Elbe and the Danube. The river valleys were old trade routes across Europe. Many roads and railways still go along them, passing through the old trading towns.

The German people

Many different groups of people live in Germany and some areas are named after them. The Frisians live by the North Sea. Central Germany is the home of the Saxons and Thuringians. Franconians and Bavarians live in the south. They all have different ways of speaking German.

Towns and cities

Most Germans live in towns. There are over 80 towns with more than 100,000 people. More than a million people live in three big cities, Berlin, Hamburg and Munich.

Berlin is the capital of Germany. The centre of government is in Bonn. The oldest towns were founded by the Romans, over 2,000 years ago.

Germany at work

Germany is an industrial nation and is the world's third largest manufacturer, after the United States and Japan. Half of the working people have jobs in factories. They make cars, computers, electrical goods and chemical products.

Germany is Europe's biggest car maker and produces about 4 million cars a year.

Mines and electricity

Germany imports most of the materials it needs for its factories from other countries. It has its own coal, soft brown coal and salt mines.

It has some natural gas and oil. Its electricity comes from hydroelectric dams and nuclear power stations.

Trains and planes

Germany's first railway was built in 1835 between Nuremberg and Fürth. It was 6 km (3½ miles) long. Today, Germany's railway lines are so long they would reach all around the world. There are about 12 big airports. One of the biggest in the world is at Frankfurt and is used by 25 million passengers a year.

On the land

Forests cover about a third of Germany. About half of the country is used to grow food and rear animals for meat and milk. The main crops are potatoes, sugar beet and cereals such as wheat, barley and rye. There are great orchards of fruit trees in Germany. Germans grow the most hops in the world. Hops are used to make beer.

natural gas

Holland

Brussels

Belgium

Bonn

Luxembourg

France

Duisburg

Dort

Düsseldorf
Ford

Cologne

Taun

Frank

Eifel

Rhine

chemic

Saarbrücken

Strasbourg

Rhine

Switzerland

Plains and mountains

The country is flat in the north. In the centre of Germany, there are mountains up to 1,500 m (5,000 ft) high. Some of the highest mountains are Feldberg in the Black Forest, Arber in the Bavarian Forest and Fichtelberg in a mountain range called the Erzgebirge. In the Alps, there are mountains over 2,000 m (6,500 ft) high. Zugspitze is Germany's tallest mountain and is almost 3,000 m (10,000 ft) high.

Looking at the map

Germany lies in the middle of Europe, as you can see from the little map at the bottom of this page. On the big map, you can find the main cities, the railways, the motorways and the airports.

Look at the little pictures below and then find them on the big map. They show you where the Germans grow their food, make wine and beer, and have their factories.

cereals
wine
coal
sugar beet
brown coal
fruit
airports
hops
nuclear power stations
potatoes
farm animals
motorways
railways

Germany in Europe

3

On the north coast

There are two seas on the north coast of Germany, the North Sea and the Baltic. The North Sea is very dirty because so much waste from towns and factories is carried to it by rivers. It is often very stormy in autumn and winter. When there is a storm at the same time as a high tide, the sea may break down the sea walls on the shore and flood the land.

The island of Sylt is a good place for summer holidays.

ancient sto

The Halligens are low islands off the coast. Some have only one farm. At high tide, they are only just above the water.

lifeboat

Schleswig Holstein

Big ships sail along this canal which joins the North Sea to the Baltic Sea.

The island of Helgoland in the North Sea has high, red cliffs. Thousands of seabirds nest on the cliffs. Many tourists come by boat to see them.

sand yachting

Kiel Canal

East Frisian Islands

Cuxhaven

Bremer-haven

Many artists live on the moors near Worpswede.

Wilhelmshaven

Bremen

Weser

Walls, called dykes, have been built along the coast. They hold back the sea and stop it from flooding the land at high tide.

Bremen is a very old city and port on the River Weser. It is also famous for a fairy tale about an old donkey, a dog, a cat and a cockerel which scared some robbers.

Hamburg
Berlin
Bonn
Dresden
Munich

Luneberg Heath is a large, sandy nature reserve where animals and plants are protected. At the end of summer, the whole heath is pink with heather. Shepherds look after flocks of black-faced moorland sheep.

Celle

The Baltic Sea

The Baltic is not so stormy as the North Sea and the water is not so salty. It is much safer for swimming. But because even more waste from cities and factories is carried to it by the rivers, it is even dirtier than the North Sea.

chalk cliffs

Rügen is the largest and most beautiful of the German islands. The island is famous for its white cliffs.

amber

Kiel is a large port.

A long bridge joins the island of Fehmarn to the mainland.

Lübeck

Lübeck is famous for marzipan.

Rostock is a port with big shipyards.

Amber, which is resin from ancient fir trees, is found on the shore.

Anklam

Otto Lilienthal, who made the first gliders, was born in Anklam in 1848.

Mecklenberg is an area of low hills and many lakes. Here the fields are yellow with crops of rape. This is grown for its oil and for feeding animals.

Schwerin

Hamburg is the second largest city in Germany, with over 1½ million people. Although it is 100 km (60 miles) from the sea, it is Germany's biggest port. Ships sail from the North Sea up the River Elbe to the city.

Mecklenburg lake district

Uckermark

Neustrelitz

Elbe

Uelzen

Wittenberge

Salzwedel

This is a giant lift for ships. It is at Niederfinow. It raises ships on the River Oder 36 m (118 ft) up to the Oder-Havel Canal.

Central Germany

Central Germany lies between two big rivers, the Weser and the Elbe. They are linked by the Mittelland Canal. Here there is all sorts of countryside, from low plains to high mountains. The highest mountains are in the Harz and Erz ranges and in the Thuringian forest.

Celle

Special horse called Hanoverians, are bred near the town of Celle.

Hanover is the capital of lower Saxony. Every year a fair for all kinds of technology is held here.

Weser

Minden

Harz

Near Minden, a bridge carries the Mittelland Canal over the River Elbe.

Bielefeld

Teutoburg Forest

Hamelin

Boden-Werder

Paderborn is an old market and cathedral town. It is now famous for its computer industry.

The Pied Piper of Hamelin played his pipe here. Baron Münchhausen, who told stories, lived in Bodenwerder.

Weser

Brocken is the highest mountain in the Harz range. On one night a year, so the story goes, witches ride there on broomsticks.

Kassel

Behind the Edertal dam is a huge reservoir.

Wartburg

Rothaargebirge

In the university town of Marburg, is the oldest medieval church in Germany.

These are traditional Schwalm costumes.

Martin Luther was a religious reformer. He translated the Bible at Wartburg in 1521.

Siegen

Germany is one of the world's leading glider builders.

Westerwald

Vogelsberg

This area is famous for gliding.

Wasser-kuppe

Dolls have been made at Sonneberg for 200 years. In the toy museum there are toys from all over the world.

Spessart Inn was once a highwaymen's den, or so an old story says. They robbed people travelling through the forests.

Rhön

Hamburg

Berlin

Main

Schweinfurt

Bonn

Dresden

Aschaffen-burg

Munich

Spessart

The old town of Schweinfurt was built at a ford, a shallow crossing place on the River Main. It is now famous for making wheels and ballbearings.

After the Second World War, Germany was divided into two separate states in 1949. They were known as East Germany and West Germany.

The capital Berlin was also divided, by a huge wall, into East Berlin and West Berlin. In 1989, after a peaceful revolution, the East Germans pulled down the wall. The two Germanies became one state again in 1990.

Castle Sanssouci, which means "without worries", is at Potsdam, near Berlin. It was built by Frederick the Great, the King of Prussia, 250 years ago.

Sanssouci

Many branches of the River Spree run through Spree Forest. It is a good place to take river trips.

Eulenspiegel, ...man who played ...ks on people, so ... stories say, came ...m near Brunswick.

...cken

Thale

...he Kyffhaus ...untains, the ...ry says, King ...barossa waits ...Judgement ...y. A raven wakes him every ...000 years.

...enach

The salt mine at Halle, on the River Saale, is now a museum.

Halle

Soft brown coal is mined at Bitterfeld.

Leipzig

Elbe

Our poems are famous around the world.

There are statues of two famous German poets, Goethe and Schiller, in Weimar.

Jena

Glass and optical equipment is made in Jena.

Leipzig is the centre of the book trade. It is also famous for the Thomaner Choir.

Meissen is famous for its porcelain china.

Chemnitz

A card game called skat was invented at Altenburg 170 years ago.

Dresden is one of the most beautiful towns in Germany. Almost destroyed in the Second World War, it has been rebuilt. Dresden Zwinger, part of the great palace, is world famous.

Thuringer Forest

Around Saalfeld are caves like fairy grottos.

Erzgebirge

Accordions and harmonicas are made in Klingenthal.

Klingen-thal

Oberwiesenthal is the highest town in Germany. It is a good place for skiing and sledging. A cable car carries skiers 1,214 m (3,982 ft) up the mountain.

Fichtelgebirge

The composer, Richard Wagner, built an opera house in Bayreuth. Thousands of people come to the opera festivals.

Oberpfalz Forest

The River Rhine

The Rhine is Germany's biggest river and the busiest waterway in Europe. It starts in Switzerland and ends in Holland where it runs into the North Sea. In Germany, it flows along a wide valley with many old towns and cathedrals on its banks. Grapes, which are made into famous wines, grow on the slopes of the valley.

There are many round lakes in the Eifel region. They are called maars and were craters of volcanoes which filled up with water.

Between the Rhine and Ruhr rivers is Germany's "Coal Basin". Much of the country's industry is here. Many factories were built close to the huge coal mines.

la, la, la, la, la!

Many boats have crashed into the Lorelei rocks. The story says that Lorelei sits here, combing her hair and luring sailors to their deaths.

Help!

There are many old castles on the Rhine. One was built 600 years ago in the middle of the river, near Kaub. It was a toll station. Ships had to stop here to pay a toll, or money, to use the river.

Cuckoo clocks, which go "cuckoo" instead of striking, are made in the Black Forest. The hills around Feldberg are good places for holidays. But the pine forests are dying because of smoke from factories and car fumes.

At Schaffhausen in Switzerland, the Rhine plunges over cliffs in a great waterfall. It is a natural border between the two countries.

cuckoo!

Lake Constance is the largest lake in Germany. Here three countries meet. The lake also belongs to Switzerland and Austria. Fruit trees grow on its banks. People first lived here in the Stone Age, in houses on stilts in the lake.

Castle Gutenfels

castle

Binnen-hafen

Duisburg

Dortmund

Essen

Ruhr district

Düsseldorf

Cologne

Cologne Cathedral

Bonn

Koblenz

Eifel

Moselle

Kaub

Frankfurt

Mainz

Main

Bingen

Mäuse-turm

Heidelberg

Rhine

Karlsruhe

Black Forest

Danube

Schaffhausen

Mang-turm

Lindau

Unter-Uhldingen

Meersburg

Mainau Island

Constance

Lake Constance

Between the River Main and the Danube

Many tourists visit the old famous city of Heidelberg, on the River Neckar.

This minstrel is buried in the castle.

Near Bamberg, there are cliffs and caves in the mountains. Here you can see stalagmites and stalactites.

Dürer's house

Frankfurt is the centre for banking in Germany. Goethe, the poet, was born here.

There are many vineyards around the town of Würzburg. Here you can see Marienberg Castle where a famous minstrel is buried.

The painter, Dürer, was born in the old town of Nuremberg in Bavaria.

Ships using the Main-Danube Canal can sail from the North Sea all the way to the Black Sea. Nuremberg and Bamberg are ports on the canal.

Regensburg was an important town in the Middle Ages. The singers in its famous church choir are called the "cathedral sparrows".

Goethe's house

Frankfurt

There is an artificial lake at Rothenfels.

Rothenberg still looks like a medieval town.

Stuttgart is the capital of this region. It is the centre of a large industrial area. This is where Mercedes and Porsche cars are made. The poet, Schiller, was born in the city.

At Ulm, so the story goes, a tailor tried to fly but fell into the Danube.

The first German housing estate was built at Augsburg over 470 years ago.

Three great rivers meet at Passau. Here the Ilz and Inn flow into the Danube. Passau is called Germany's Venice.

Main
Schweinfurt
Würzberg
Bamberg
Fränkische Schweiz
Main-Danube Canal
Mannheim
Heidelberg
Neckar
Schiller
Rhine
Nuremberg
Altmühl
Stuttgart
Tübingen
Donauwörth
Ingolstadt
Regensburg
Isar
Danube
Passau
Inn
Landshut
Ulm
Danube
Iller
Lech
Augsburg
Hamburg
Berlin
Bonn Dresden
Munich

In the Alps

In southern Germany are high mountains, the Alps. Thick forests grow on the slopes and there is snow on the tops all the year.

Many of the houses in Bavaria have paintings on the outside walls. These tell all sorts of stories in pictures.

Marmots, chamois and golden eagles live high up in the Alps. Alpine roses, blue gentians, edelweiss and thistles flower among the rocks.

There are big ski jumps in Obertsdorf and Garmisch.

Hang gliders take off from the high peaks.

Neuschwanstein is like a fairy tale castle. It was built by King Ludwig II. Millions of tourists visit it each year.

Yodelayeedee!

In autumn, farmers bring their cows down from the high fields to the valleys for the winter.

At Berchtesgaden you can visit a deep salt mine.

Allgäu Alps

Zugspitze

Ammer-See

Starnberger See

Munich

Isar

Chiemsee

Mountain climber

Königs-see

Every ten years, the people in Oberammergau act in a play about Christ and Easter.

Museum

Violins are made in Mittenwald. There is a school for violin makers and a special violin museum.

Hamburg
Berlin
Bonn Dresden
Munich

Walchensee

Kochelsee

Water from one lake, the Walchensee, flows down to another lake, the Kochelsee. It goes through a power station, making electricity.

German towns

The oldest towns in Germany were built by the Romans. Many towns were started in the Middle Ages but they were much smaller than towns today.

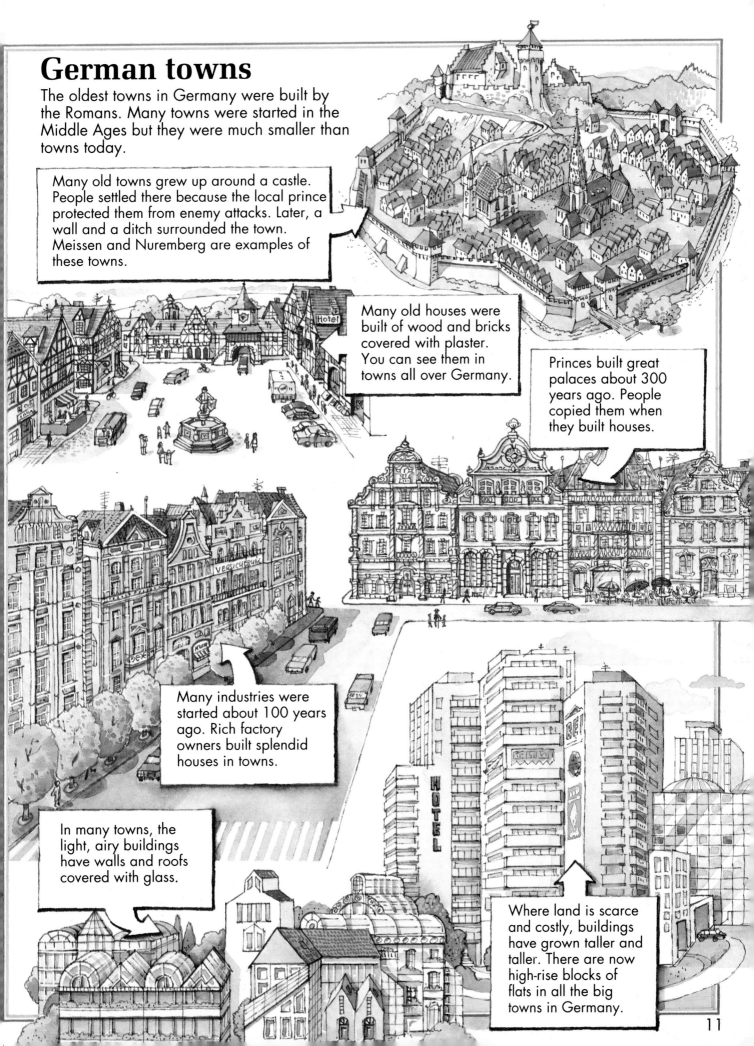

Many old towns grew up around a castle. People settled there because the local prince protected them from enemy attacks. Later, a wall and a ditch surrounded the town. Meissen and Nuremberg are examples of these towns.

Many old houses were built of wood and bricks covered with plaster. You can see them in towns all over Germany.

Princes built great palaces about 300 years ago. People copied them when they built houses.

Many industries were started about 100 years ago. Rich factory owners built splendid houses in towns.

In many towns, the light, airy buildings have walls and roofs covered with glass.

Where land is scarce and costly, buildings have grown taller and taller. There are now high-rise blocks of flats in all the big towns in Germany.

Houses and clothes

In each of the different areas of Germany, many of the farmhouses all look the same. They have been built in the same way for hundreds of years. The people who lived in these different areas used to wear traditional costumes. Now very few people wear these special clothes but they still have their own way of speaking German.

On the North Sea coast of Schleswig-Holstein and on the Frisian Islands, the farmhouses have roofs thatched with reeds. The walls are built of bricks.

People live in the front part of the house, next to the barn or stable where the animals are kept.

Take an umbrella. It may rain.

If you shout in the Black Forest you can often hear an echo.

Farmhouses in the Alps in Upper Bavaria are built of stone and wood. The family lives at the front. Cows are kept in a barn at the back, with a hayloft over it.

In winter the snow stays on the wide roof, keeping the house warm. Stones on the roof stop the wind from blowing the wooden tiles away.

In the Black Forest, farmhouses are built mostly of wood and have a wooden balcony. The steep roof is covered with wooden tiles.

The farmer lives on the ground floor, with barns at the back. Above is the hayloft. The farmer drives his haycart up a ramp at the back and into the loft.

We build our farmhouses in valleys or on sunny slopes.

You can see these wood and brick houses over Lower Saxony in northern Germany. They are called "half-timbered" and they are thatched with reeds. The family lives in the middle of the house and the barn is at the side.

The crossed horses' heads at the top of the roof keep away evil spirits, or so says an old German belief.

These are our traditional costumes but we usually wear jeans!

In Mark Brandenburg you can see houses like this. In the past, the farmer drove his cart under the covered part at the front. He could work there, out of the wind and rain. Farmers in this sandy area now grow mostly cereals, sugar beet and potatoes.

In the summer, it's very warm and sunny in the mountains.

We'll eat dumplings and sausages at our wedding party.

You can find small farms like this in central and western Germany. The house, cow sheds and barns were built around a three-sided yard. To get to the farm you have to drive through a gate. In the old days, the farmer threshed the cereals, to take off the husks, in the yard.

In many of the big towns in Germany, whole families all wear the same kind of modern clothes. The new blocks of flats look the same in every town. It is only when people speak that Germans can tell they come from a different part of Germany.

Most people live in cities.

Town and country

Three-quarters of all German people live and work in towns. Only farmers still work in the country.

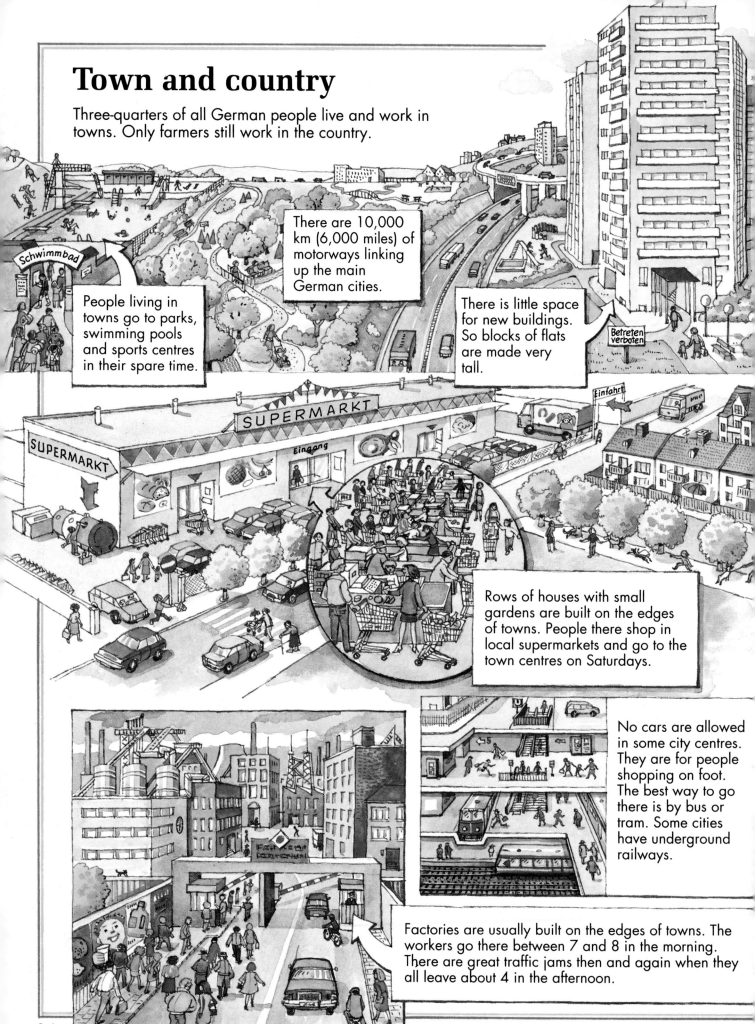

There are 10,000 km (6,000 miles) of motorways linking up the main German cities.

People living in towns go to parks, swimming pools and sports centres in their spare time.

There is little space for new buildings. So blocks of flats are made very tall.

Rows of houses with small gardens are built on the edges of towns. People there shop in local supermarkets and go to the town centres on Saturdays.

No cars are allowed in some city centres. They are for people shopping on foot. The best way to go there is by bus or tram. Some cities have underground railways.

Factories are usually built on the edges of towns. The workers go there between 7 and 8 in the morning. There are great traffic jams then and again when they all leave about 4 in the afternoon.

Living in the country is often nicer than living in a town. Many people have houses with big gardens. Children can play in the streets because there is not much traffic. Buses take them to and from the schools.

Most villages have a post office. In the past, the mail came by coach and the horses were changed at inns. They are still called post inns.

Modern farm

In the middle of a village is the church. It has a cemetery, usually with a wall around it.

People in a village buy things at the shop. But these are closing down because supermarkets have become popular.

Gasthof zur Post

EMMA STEIN

EIS

Many farmers have sold their small farms or turned them into holiday homes or riding stables. People from the towns come for holidays here.

PONYHOF

Altdor

Today, there are very few farmhouses, like the one shown here, in German villages. Farmers have joined together to make bigger farms and built new ones outside the villages.

15

Anna's day

Anna is an ordinary German girl. Many German children spend their days just like Anna. Anna's father goes to his office in the morning and comes back again in the evening. Her mother works part-time so she is at home when Anna comes back from school.

Anna is 8 years old and is in the third year at her primary school. She gets up every day just before 7 am and has her breakfast at quarter past, if she hasn't overslept again.

woof woof

Anna goes on the school bus with other children who live near her. It leaves on the dot of 7.30 am. Anna is usually the last one on. The driver does not wait for her if she is late.

Special days

When there is a christening, the family and friends go to the church. The godmother holds the baby during the service.

When they are 9, Catholic children go to their first Communion.

Protestant children are confirmed at 14.

Every time Anna misses the bus, she has to walk all the way. Then she is late for school and the lessons have started when she gets there. The teacher is always quite cross with her.

All children have to stay at school until they are 15. Then some leave and others go on to further education.

Good! That's school over for today.

At 1 o'clock, Anna goes home. Some children stay on until 4 pm because there is no one at home.

Anna's birthday party

When Anna had a birthday party, she asked lots of her friends. Here are some of the games they played.

I won!

Sack racing

Sausage snapping

Blind man's buff

After school

howl!

STRUPPI

Violin lessons

Piano lessons

Homework

Where's the ball?

After school, Anna is very busy. She is learning to play the violin and the piano, and has to practise. She is also learning to play tennis.

Your lolly or your life!

Anna's hobby is her computer. She does her homework on it. She enjoys playing computer games. She also likes to read and watch television. She likes detective films best.

At 7.30 pm, the family has supper. They have all had a hot lunch, so supper is usually cold. They eat bread, cold meats, cheese and salad, and some fruit. Soon after supper, Anna has to go to bed. She often reads until 9 pm.

Sonntag 13

On Sundays, Anna can get up late and have breakfast with her mother and father. On Sunday afternoons, Anna's granny and cousin often come for coffee and cakes. The whole family sometimes go for a drive in the country.

Sports and activities

Germans like to play all kinds of sports and games at weekends, and when they are on holiday. Some people join sports clubs and many watch sports programmes on television.

In winter, people go skiing and bob-sleigh racing on the mountains. They go cross-country skiing on the lower slopes. Many children skate, specially in north Germany.

Many sports, specially football, tennis, ice hockey and car racing, are shown on television. Sometimes the whole family watches sport together at the weekends. National league football matches are played on Saturdays and are very popular.

Goal!

In summer, everyone likes to go out for the day. Children living in towns go to the swimming pools. Children in the country swim in lakes and rivers. Some families drive to the seaside where they swim or go boating.

Many children go cycling or walking with their parents in their spare time. Some fly kites or model aeroplanes. Others play hopscotch or table tennis, or go skateboarding. They also like playing board games, such as draughts and chess.

18

In Hansa park at Sierksdorf, the water slides are 80 m (262 ft) high.

The bird zoo at Walsrode, near Hanover, is the biggest in the world.

At Cottbus you can play with a real train. Here the little railway is run by children.

In Heidepark at Soltau, there is a display of alligators and a giant roller-coaster with four loops.

At the Duisburg Zoo, whales and dolphins show off their tricks.

There are thousands of things to see and do in Germany. There are nearly a hundred zoos and wildlife parks. Berlin has two zoos. The one in the eastern part of the city is the biggest in Germany. The one in the western part has more different kinds of animals than any zoo in Europe. There are also over fifty adventure and theme parks. There you can watch performing animals or ride on roller-coasters and big dippers. In many theme parks you can ride ponies.

You can see models of dinosaurs at the Geiselwind theme park.

At Geiselgasteig, near Munich, you can see film sets.

At the Europa park, near Freiberg, you can have space rides.

The game many children in Germany like playing best is ludo. It is played on a board marked with coloured squares and a dice. The four players each have four coloured pieces and move them after throwing the dice. The first player to move round the board wins.

Food and drink

German food is good, filling and often tastes quite different from British food. Pork is the favourite meat in Germany and there are lots of different kinds of sausages, eaten hot or cold. Each region has its own way of cooking meat and potatoes. Adults drink mineral water, beer and wine. Children like fizzy drinks, milk and fruit juice.

He'll never eat all that!

Breakfast

Coffee, tea, milk or cocoa, black bread, bread rolls, butter, jam and sometimes a boiled egg.

Lunch

This could be pork, sauerkraut (pickled cabbage), and potatoes, and chocolate blancmange.

Supper

Cold meats, cheese, bread and tomatoes. Beer for adults, juice for children.

Recipe for Arme Ritter (Poor Knights)
For 4 people:
8 slices stale white bread
1/3 litre (3/4 pint) milk
2 eggs, pinch of salt
breadcrumbs
fat for frying

Mix the milk and eggs, pour over the bread. Leave to soak.

Sprinkle with breadcrumbs.

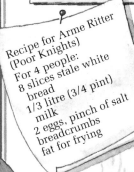

Fry in hot fat until brown on both sides.

Eat them hot!

Yummy!

I like sugar, lemon and cinnamon on mine.

Ich kann kochen

German food

Bread rolls are very popular in Germany and there are many different kinds. They are often covered in poppy seeds or caraway seeds.

Most Germans like meatballs and meat loaves of all kinds which they eat with special sauces.

Potato dishes are a German favourite. Potato dumplings are balls of potato mixed with egg, salt and flour which are cooked in salted water.

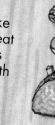
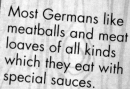
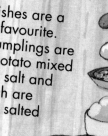

Some German dishes

Smoked herrings

Pickled herrings

Meatballs in a sauce, with a red berry jelly.

Pickled eggs

Labskaus is a stew made of potatoes, beetroot, salt beef and salt herrings.

Kohl und Pinkel, from Lower Saxony, is cabbage with bacon and sausage.

Pork knuckle with peas is a Berlin speciality. Eggs are pickled in brine.

Jam doughnut

Himmel und Erde (heaven and earth) is potatoes, apples, onions and black pudding.

Himmelreich (kingdom of heaven) is pork, prunes, sauce and dumplings.

Reibekuchen are fried potato cakes, which are eaten with apple sauce.

In Frankfurt people eat a special cheese with onions, and frankfurters. They drink apple wine.

Potato dumplings go well with roast meat.

In Leipzig, they eat vegetables with slices of cold meat.

These little fish are caught in the River Main.

This is a dish of sausages cooked in wine.

People in Bavaria eat bread dumplings with mushrooms.

These noodles are made of cooked potatoes.

This big sausage is filled with potatoes, onions and minced meat.

Bavarian snacks:

Fish on sticks

Black Forest ham

Senf

Meat loaf with eggs.

Black Forest gateau

Bavarian leg of pork with dumplings and pickled cabbage.

White radish

A stew made of savoy cabbage, other vegetables and different kinds of meat.

This is a pasta, served with grated cheese and fried onions.

Festivals and customs

Many places in Germany have big religious festivals which are held every year. There are also national holidays and traditional customs.

On 6 January, singers carrying stars celebrate the coming of the Three Kings.

6 January

A big carnival is held in February. It is a very old custom. People wear fancy dress and masks.

February

At Easter, there are hunts for Easter eggs.

March or April

In the south, people dance around a maypole on 1 May.

May Day

On Corpus Christi Day, Catholics hold processions in the streets.

May or June

People light big bonfires on Midsummer's Eve.

24 June

In Bavaria, people ride on horses and in carts on the feast day of St. Leonhard.

November

On their first day at school, children are given paper cones full of sweets.

August or September

On Martinma, children carr paper lantern they have made

November

At Christmas in the south, the Christchild brings presents. In the north it is Father Christmas.

I don't want that!

24 December

On the night before his special day, St. Nicholas fills children's boots with sweets and goodies.

6 December

On New Year's Eve, there are firework displays. People drop hot lead into water and tell their fortunes.

New Year's Eve

At Bremen there is an old custom. A little tailor has to test the ice on the River Weser.

It looks solid.

On the Monday before Ash Wednesday, there are big carnivals in Mainz, Cologne and Düsseldorf. People put on fancy dress.

A play of the story is put on at the Pied Piper of Hamelin festival.

On 22 February, fires are lit on the North Frisian Islands. This was to light whaling boats going to sea.

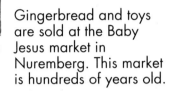

Gingerbread and toys are sold at the Baby Jesus market in Nuremberg. This market is hundreds of years old.

The fried fish festival at Worms lasts for nine days. The fishermen have mock battles in Floss harbour.

The children's carnival at Dinklesbühl remembers the Thirty Years' War. It ended in 1648. During the war, the children persuaded the Swedish army not to destroy their town.

Every four years, the people of Landshut go back in time to the Middle Ages. They dress up and hold a feast to remember the marriage of a local nobleman to a Polish princess.

The Munich beer festival begins at the end of September. It was first held in 1811 and is now the biggest festival in the world. Over 6 million visitors come to Munich.

On a Saturday in July, there is a town festival in Memmingen. People go in for a fishing competition. The one who catches the biggest fish is King of the Fishermen.

Look! I'll be King of the Fishermen.

In the winter, there are exciting sledge races in Bavaria. Everyone rides on old-fashioned woodcutters' sledges.

Things to see

Every year millions of visitors go to Germany. Many spend their holidays in the mountains or by the sea. Some tour around the country looking at the many interesting things.

At the aquarium in Kiel, you can see the wildlife which lives in the North Sea and the Baltic.

Seabirds breed in the Watt national park and migrating birds rest there.

In the area around Münster, there are hundreds of wonderful old castles. They have moats with bridges across.

Wild horses live in the marshes near Dülmen. They are rounded up each year.

The town of Xanten, on the River Rhine, was founded by the Romans. Here you can see an Ancient Roman temple and an amphitheatre.

Many people go to watch racing cars roar over the Nürburg track in the Eifel region.

At Wuppertal, you can travel around the town on an overhead railway. The first railway was built over 90 years ago.

The biggest moving radio telescope in the world is near Effelsberg.

100 metres (328 ft.)

You can see models of dinosaur skeletons in the Senckenberg Museum in Frankfurt.

Ulm Cathedral has the world's highest church tower, with 758 steps.

In the Friedrichshafen Museum on Lake Constance are models of airships.

You can go on a mountain railway or in a cable car to the top of Germany's highest mountain, Zugspitze.

Rhine

HINDENBURG

In Bad Segeburg there are open-air plays about the Wild West, based on the stories of Karl May, best-selling author.

3

4 There is a museum all about ships at Rostock.

5 Berlin has over 50 museums. In one is the statue of the Ancient Egyptian queen, Nefertiti. You can also see many famous paintings.

6 In the Harz mountains there are huge caves. They are full of stalagmites and stalactites.

16 There is a huge reservoir behind the Bleiloch dam on the river Saale. The wall is 200 m (656 ft) long.

Buchenwald was a concentration camp. It has a memorial to the thousands of people who were killed here. **11**

12 At Radebeul, near Dresden, there is an American Indian museum. It is at Villa Barenfett (villa bear's fat).

14 Wooden toys are made at Seiffen in the Erz mountains.

15 In the Erz mountains is a museum called the Hammer of Frohnau. You can see how iron ore was worked there.

13 The Bastei are sandstone cliffs, 300 m (984 ft) high, on the River Elbe. Rock climbers practise on the hundreds of cliffs.

17 In the castle at Coburg, there are art galleries and an armour exhibition.

24 Munich has over 30 museums. The German Museum has the world's biggest display of technology.

25 A fairy-tale castle was built by the Bavarian King, Ludwig II, on an island in the Chiemsee.

23 In the Bavarian Forest national park animals in danger of extinction live in the wild. There are some lynx and wolves.

Elbe

Main

Danube

The story of Germany

The first accounts of Germany came from the Romans who tried to conquer the region over 2,000 years ago. They came upon tribes of people living by hunting and farming. The Romans called the tribes' land Germania.

2nd Century

About 1,900 years ago, the Romans built the Limes, a wooden wall and ditch, to keep the tribes out of the Roman empire.

5th Century

Many of the tribes moved south and invaded the area that had been conquered by the Romans. They broke up a part of the Roman empire into tribal kingdoms. The kingdom of the Franks became the most important.

You can still see many Roman buildings, such as the Porta Nigra in Trier.

Monastery

768 - 814 Charlemagne founded the empire of the Franks. He built palaces, monasteries and schools all over his huge empire.

The Emperor's Palace

at Ingelheim on the River Rhine.

The Crusaders marched to Jerusalem. They wanted to capture the Holy City and drive out the non-Christians.

During his reign, Charlemagne conquered most of central and western Europe. When he died, his empire split up into many small kingdoms, each with its own ruler and government. Many rulers tried to unite the kingdoms into an empire again but it never lasted for long.

12th Century

Knights had to fight for their king and supply their own armour and horses.

Many people moved from the country to live near the castles. They felt safe from attack there. They built the first towns.

13th Century

14th Century

Craftsmen and merchants in north Germany formed a league so they could trade with foreign lands. Their ships sailed around the North Sea and the Baltic.

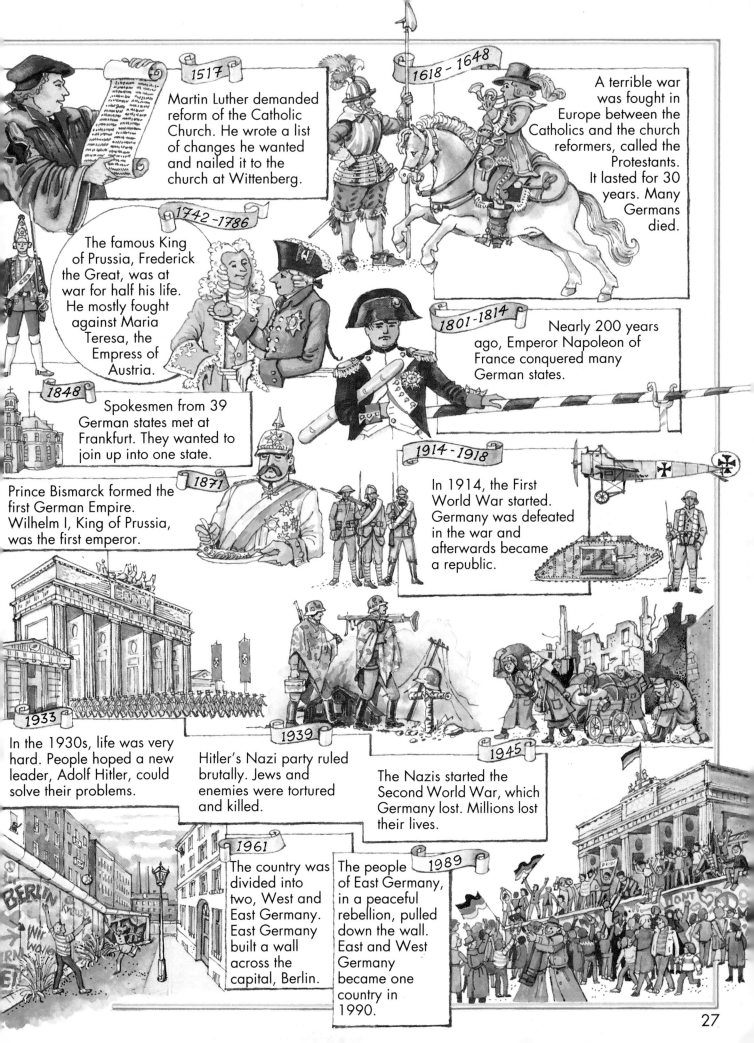

1517
Martin Luther demanded reform of the Catholic Church. He wrote a list of changes he wanted and nailed it to the church at Wittenberg.

1618 – 1648
A terrible war was fought in Europe between the Catholics and the church reformers, called the Protestants. It lasted for 30 years. Many Germans died.

1742 –1786
The famous King of Prussia, Frederick the Great, was at war for half his life. He mostly fought against Maria Teresa, the Empress of Austria.

1801-1814
Nearly 200 years ago, Emperor Napoleon of France conquered many German states.

1848
Spokesmen from 39 German states met at Frankfurt. They wanted to join up into one state.

1871
Prince Bismarck formed the first German Empire. Wilhelm I, King of Prussia, was the first emperor.

1914 - 1918
In 1914, the First World War started. Germany was defeated in the war and afterwards became a republic.

1933
In the 1930s, life was very hard. People hoped a new leader, Adolf Hitler, could solve their problems.

1939
Hitler's Nazi party ruled brutally. Jews and enemies were tortured and killed.

1945
The Nazis started the Second World War, which Germany lost. Millions lost their lives.

1961
The country was divided into two, West and East Germany. East Germany built a wall across the capital, Berlin.

1989
The people of East Germany, in a peaceful rebellion, pulled down the wall. East and West Germany became one country in 1990.

Famous German people

Hey, that's our rabbit!

The first famous German was Neanderthal Man. The Neanderthals lived about 40,000 years ago in central Europe. Remains of them were found in 1856 near Düsseldorf.

Characters in German fairy tales are famous all around the world.

This golden statue is said to be of Barbarossa. He was an emperor in the Middle Ages.

Albrecht Dürer

Albrecht Dürer lived in Nuremberg from 1471 until 1528. He was the best-known painter in Germany.

Johann Seb. Bach *Ludwig van Beethoven*

Music composed by Bach (1685-1750) and Beethoven (1770-1827) is played all over the world.

Johann Wolfgang von Goethe *Friedrich von Schiller*

Goethe and Schiller are famous German poets. Children have to learn their poems at school.

Annette von Droste-Hülshoff was born in a castle. She was one of the first German women poets and wrote many poems and songs.

The brothers Grimm collected and wrote down hundreds of old fairy tales.

Carl Spitzweg lived in Munich in the 19th century. He painted funny pictures of the townspeople.

Clara Schumann was a famous pianist. Very few women played in public in the 19th century.

Käthe Kollwitz, a painter and sculptress, painted interesting pictures of working people.

Paula Modersohn-Becker painted many pictures of children.

Anne Frank was a German-Jewish girl who hid from the Nazis for three years in a Dutch warehouse. There she wrote her famous Diary. She was 16 when she was caught and killed in 1944.

Erich Kästner wrote many children's stories. You may have read Emil and the Detectives.

Now we'll follow him.

Other famous German things:

Garden gnomes were copied from stone figures in Turkey.

Why don't you get on with your work?

Over 20 million Volkswagen Beetle cars had been made by 1980.

We're two very naughty twins invented by Wilhelm Busch.

Max and Moritz

Heinrich Hoffmann wrote about a boy called Struwwelpeter. These children's stories are very well-known in Germany.

I'm Pumuckl - a cartoon character.

Hats and leather trousers are traditional in Bavaria.

German athletes

Franz Beckenbauer is Germany's most famous footballer. He was manager of the German team.

If only I had played...

...si Mittermaier, Germany's ...st known women skier, won ...o Olympic gold medals in ...74.

Michael Gross, a famous German swimmer, has set world records.

You won't get that one.

Boris Becker and Steffi Graf are star German tennis players. They have both been ranked number one in the world.

Famous inventors

In 1885, Carl Benz invented the first car powered by the petrol engine.

How do I get it into reverse?

In 1445, Johann Gutenberg invented the first successful printing press. He made letters which could be used over and over again.

Now I'll get my sums right!

Conrad Röntgen discovered X-rays in 1895. He was awarded the first Nobel Prize for Physics in 1901.

In 1941 Konrad Zuse from Berlin built the first electronic calculator. It was huge and weighed over 3 tonnes.

woof woof!

German facts and numbers

The German flag is black, red and gold. German soldiers had this flag when they fought against Napoleon's invading armies.

Amazing facts

Leipzig has the biggest railway station in Europe, with 26 platforms.

This special train goes at over 400 km (248 miles) an hour.

Germany's tallest town hall is in Essen. It is 106 m (347 ft) high.

The atomic clock at Brunswick keeps the most accurate time in Germany.

The Olympic Stadium at Munich has a special plexiglass roof covering the seating area.

The deepest hole is in the Oberpfalz area. A drill goes down 15 km (9 miles).

There are 120 million hens in Germany. That is 1½ hens for every German.

If all the dogs in Germany stood nose to tail, the line would stretch from London to Gibraltar.

In Germany, there are 7 million cats. They are all afraid of the 5 million dogs!

There are so many pigs in Germany, everyone could have half a pig each to eat.

There are half as many cage birds as there are German people!

There are 50 million fish in tanks and aquariums.

There are about 20 million cows in Germany, or one cow to every four people.

If you divided everyone up evenly between all the cars, there would be 2 ½ people sitting in each car.

German money is called Deutschmarks, or D-marks or DM for short, and pfennigs. There are 100 pfennigs to a Deutschmark. Here you can see some of the coins and notes.

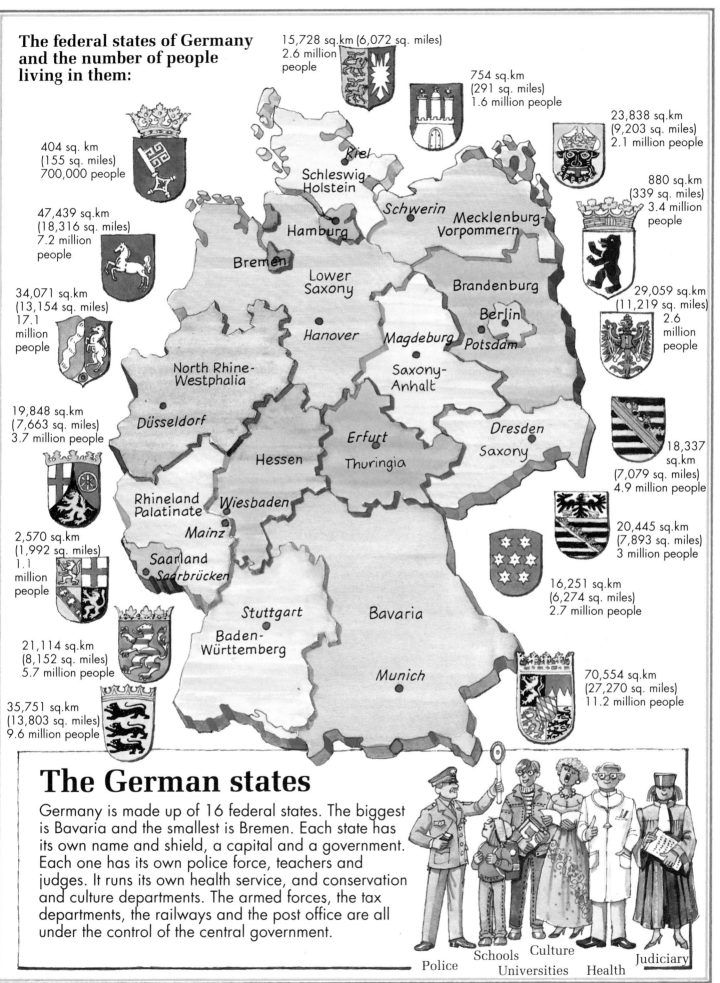

The federal states of Germany and the number of people living in them:

15,728 sq.km (6,072 sq. miles)
2.6 million people

754 sq.km (291 sq. miles)
1.6 million people

23,838 sq.km (9,203 sq. miles)
2.1 million people

404 sq. km (155 sq. miles)
700,000 people

880 sq.km (339 sq. miles)
3.4 million people

47,439 sq.km (18,316 sq. miles)
7.2 million people

29,059 sq.km (11,219 sq. miles)
2.6 million people

34,071 sq.km (13,154 sq. miles)
17.1 million people

19,848 sq.km (7,663 sq. miles)
3.7 million people

18,337 sq.km (7,079 sq. miles)
4.9 million people

2,570 sq.km (1,992 sq. miles)
1.1 million people

20,445 sq.km (7,893 sq. miles)
3 million people

21,114 sq.km (8,152 sq. miles)
5.7 million people

16,251 sq.km (6,274 sq. miles)
2.7 million people

35,751 sq.km (13,803 sq. miles)
9.6 million people

70,554 sq.km (27,270 sq. miles)
11.2 million people

Kiel

Schleswig-Holstein

Hamburg

Schwerin

Mecklenburg-Vorpommern

Bremen

Lower Saxony

Brandenburg

Berlin

Hanover

Magdeburg

Potsdam

North Rhine-Westphalia

Saxony-Anhalt

Düsseldorf

Dresden

Saxony

Erfurt

Hessen

Thuringia

Rhineland Palatinate

Wiesbaden

Mainz

Saarland

Saarbrücken

Stuttgart

Baden-Württemberg

Bavaria

Munich

The German states

Germany is made up of 16 federal states. The biggest is Bavaria and the smallest is Bremen. Each state has its own name and shield, a capital and a government. Each one has its own police force, teachers and judges. It runs its own health service, and conservation and culture departments. The armed forces, the tax departments, the railways and the post office are all under the control of the central government.

Police   Schools   Culture   Universities   Health   Judiciary

Index

First published in English in 1992 by Usborne Publishing Ltd, Usborne House, 83-85 Saffron Hill, London ECIN 8RT.

Copyright © 1991 ars edition, Munich

Copyright © English text 1992 Usborne Publishing Ltd.

All rights reserved.

The cover of "Emil and the Detectives" by Walter Trier on page 28 is reproduced with the kind permission of the Atrium Verlags in Zurich.

The "Pumuckl" figure on page 29 appears with the kind permission of the Buchagentur in Munich.

The name Usborne and the device are Trade Marks of Usborne Publishing Ltd.

Printed in Belgium.